Pinkalicious™
Pinkadoodles

By Victoria Kann

Drawings by Carolina Farias
based on the art of Victoria Kann
from the book *PINKALICIOUS*

HARPER FESTIVAL™
An Imprint of HarperCollinsPublishers

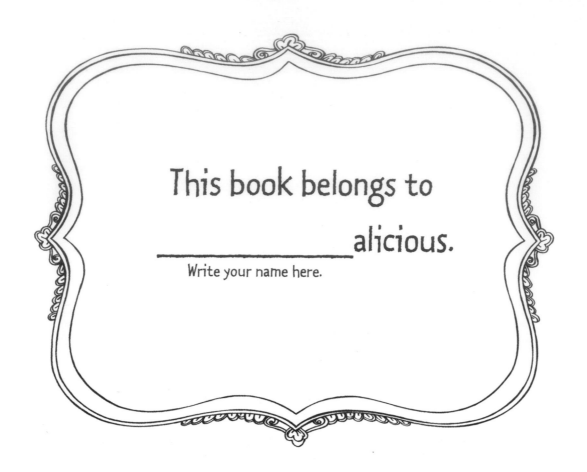

This book belongs to

_____alicious.

Write your name here.

Think Pink

My favorite color is _____!

My birthday is _____.

One day I would like to have a pet:

kitten, puppy, pony, hamster, monkey, slug

(circle as many as you want)

My favorite doll is named_____.

My favorite book is _____.

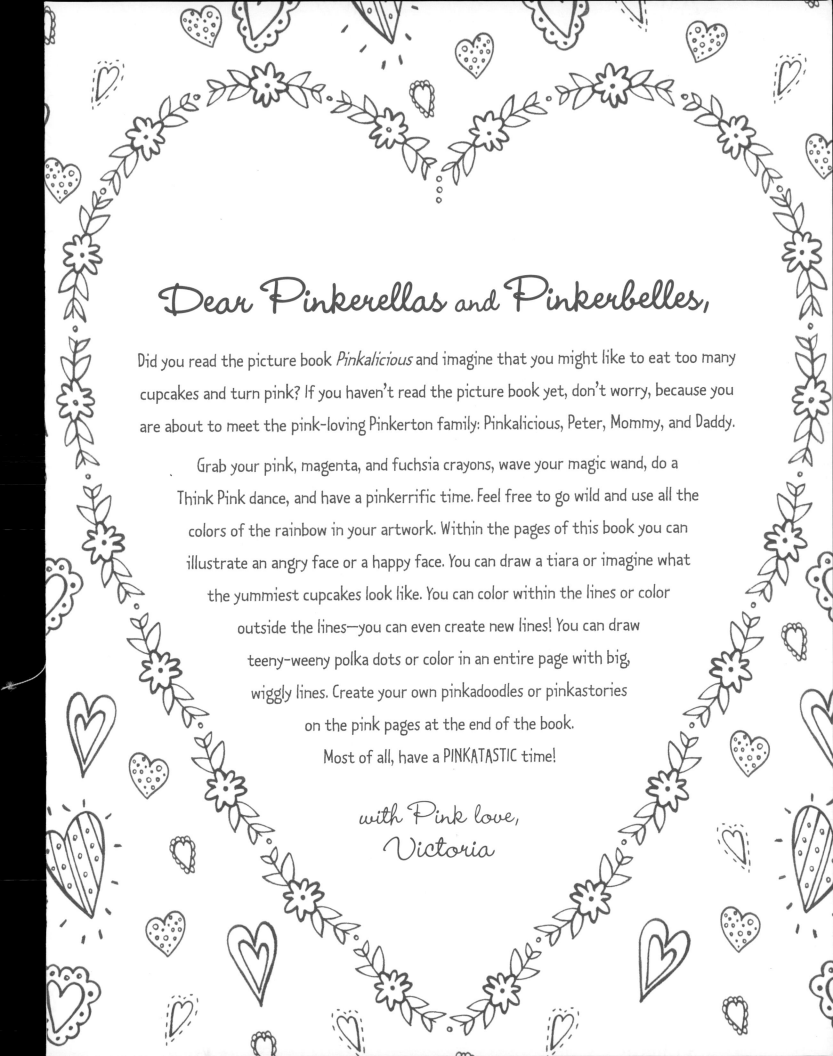

Dear Pinkerellas and Pinkerbelles,

Did you read the picture book *Pinkalicious* and imagine that you might like to eat too many cupcakes and turn pink? If you haven't read the picture book yet, don't worry, because you are about to meet the pink-loving Pinkerton family: Pinkalicious, Peter, Mommy, and Daddy.

Grab your pink, magenta, and fuchsia crayons, wave your magic wand, do a Think Pink dance, and have a pinkerrific time. Feel free to go wild and use all the colors of the rainbow in your artwork. Within the pages of this book you can illustrate an angry face or a happy face. You can draw a tiara or imagine what the yummiest cupcakes look like. You can color within the lines or color outside the lines—you can even create new lines! You can draw teeny-weeny polka dots or color in an entire page with big, wiggly lines. Create your own pinkadoodles or pinkastories on the pink pages at the end of the book.
Most of all, have a PINKATASTIC time!

with Pink love,
Victoria

Meet Pinkalicious.
Pink, pink, pink.
More than anything,
Pinkalicious loves pink,
especially pink cupcakes.
Her parents warn her
not to eat too many cupcakes,
but when Pinkalicious does . . .
she turns pink!

Pinkalicious loves the color pink!
Can you make everything on this page pink?

Draw something pinkerrific that you love.

All of these objects are pinkatastic!
Circle your favorite things.

Finish drawing the Pinkerton family.
There's Daddy, Mommy, Peter, and Pinkalicious.

Draw your family. Do they love the color pink, too?

What Are Your Favorite Colors?

The Pinkertons live in a pink house, of course.
Finish drawing the house.

Draw Your Home

What is the weather like outside?

Let's Make Cupcakes

Circle what you use when you make cupcakes
and cross out what does not belong.

Don't forget the secret ingredient!
What color do you want your cupcakes to be?
Color in the bottles!

Frost and Decorate the Cupcakes!

Draw what Pinkalicious looks like
when she is very happy.

Draw what you look like
when you are tickled pink.

What are Pinkalicious and Peter talking about?

Pink Riddle: There is a pink single-story house and everything in it is pink. The doors are pink, the windows are pink, the mirror is pink, the kitchen is pink, the chairs are pink, the table is pink, the beds are pink, even the plants are pink. What color are the stairs?

Answer: There are no stairs in a one-story house!

Which cupcake is different?

What Are Your Favorite Foods?

1 ~~~~~~~~~~~~~~~~~~~~~~~~~~~~~~~~~~~

2 ~~~~~~~~~~~~~~~~~~~~~~~~~~~~~~~~~~~

3 ~~~~~~~~~~~~~~~~~~~~~~~~~~~~~~~~~~~

4 ~~~~~~~~~~~~~~~~~~~~~~~~~~~~~~~~~~~

5 ~~~~~~~~~~~~~~~~~~~~~~~~~~~~~~~~~~~

Help Pinkalicious
furnish and decorate her room.

Add more of Pinkalicious's and Peter's favorite toys.

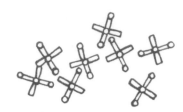

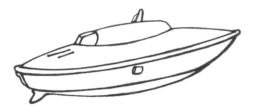

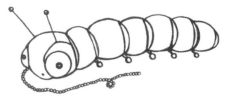

What's Your Favorite Toy?

Finish drawing the stack of cupcakes. Don't forget to decorate them!

How many have you drawn?_____

How many can you eat?_____

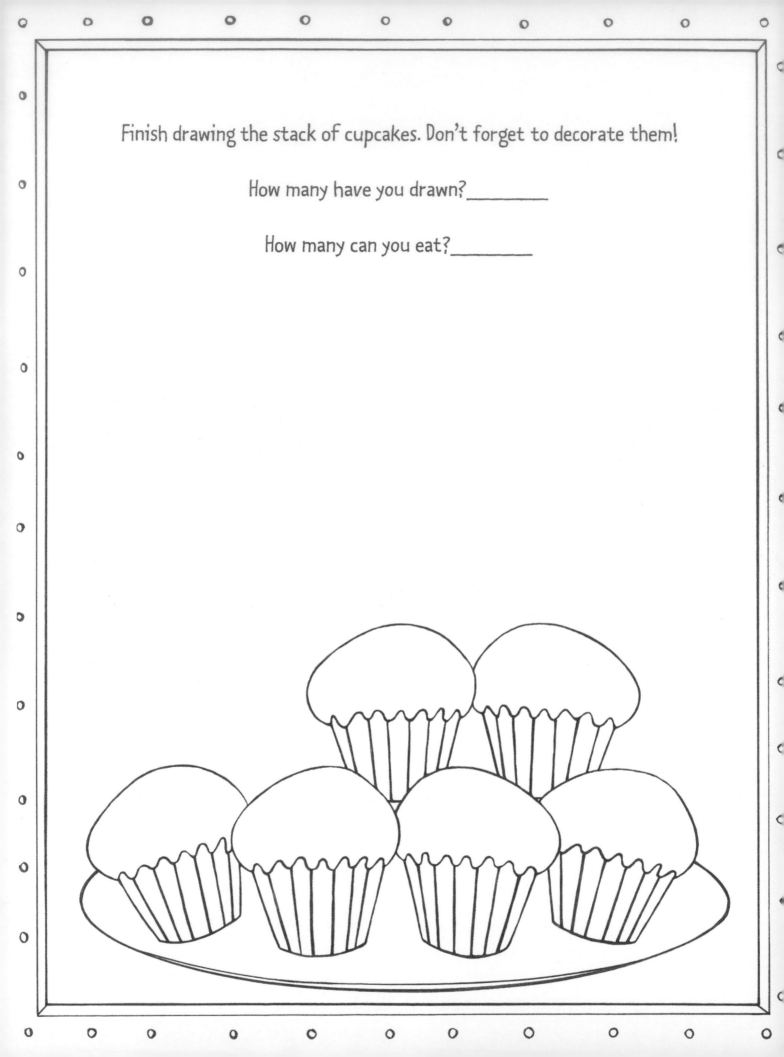

Pinkalicious likes to jump and play.
Draw yourself jumping with Pinkalicious.

What's Missing?

The vowels a, e, o, and u are missing from the sentence below.
Can you put the letters in the right places
and then read the sentence out loud?

"Y_ _ _
g_ t
wh_ t
Y_ _ _ g_ t
_nd y_ _ _
d_ n't
g_ t
_ps _ t."

Draw what Pinkalicious looks like when she's angry
that she's not allowed to eat another cupcake.

Pinkadoodle!

Can you make a picture out of these doodles?

It's bedtime for Pinkalicious.
Can you help her go to bed?

Start

Finish

Make these pajamas
absolutely pinkatastic!

Bedtime Story

Design the covers and write titles for these books.

Write a story to send
Pinkalicious and Peter off to sleep.

Once upon a Time...

_____

_____

_____

_____

_____

_____

_____

_____

_____

What is Pinkalicious dreaming
about while she sleeps?

Draw a picture of what you wish for.
Now close your eyes and count . . .

one, two, three

. . . and make your wish!

Can you color in Pinkalicious
so she turns pink?

Pinkerbelle!

Don't forget to add
her wings, wand, and crown!

Pink Tears of Happiness

Fill up the page with teardrops of all shapes and sizes.

You've turned pink!
Draw your reflection in the mirror.

How many shades of pink
can you make?

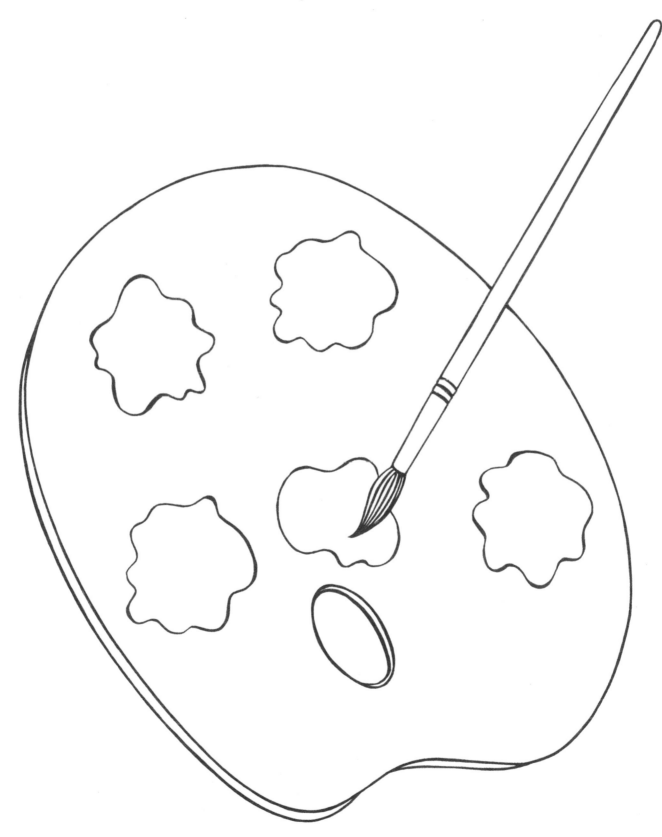

Pink Riddle: What do you call Pinkalicious in the summer?

Answer: Hot pink!

Here are Pinkalicious's favorite dress-up outfits.
Can you decorate them and draw your own?

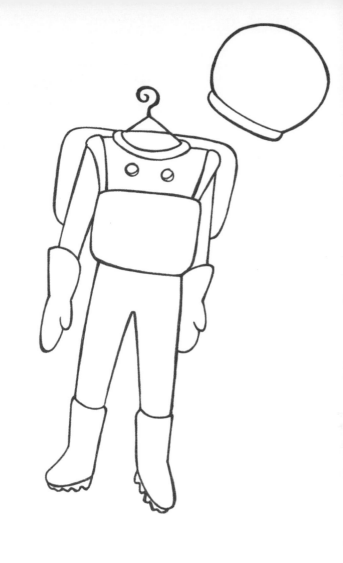

Can you change Pinkalicious's outfit
from plain to pinkatastic?
Don't forget her purse!

What is in Pinkalicious's
pink purse?

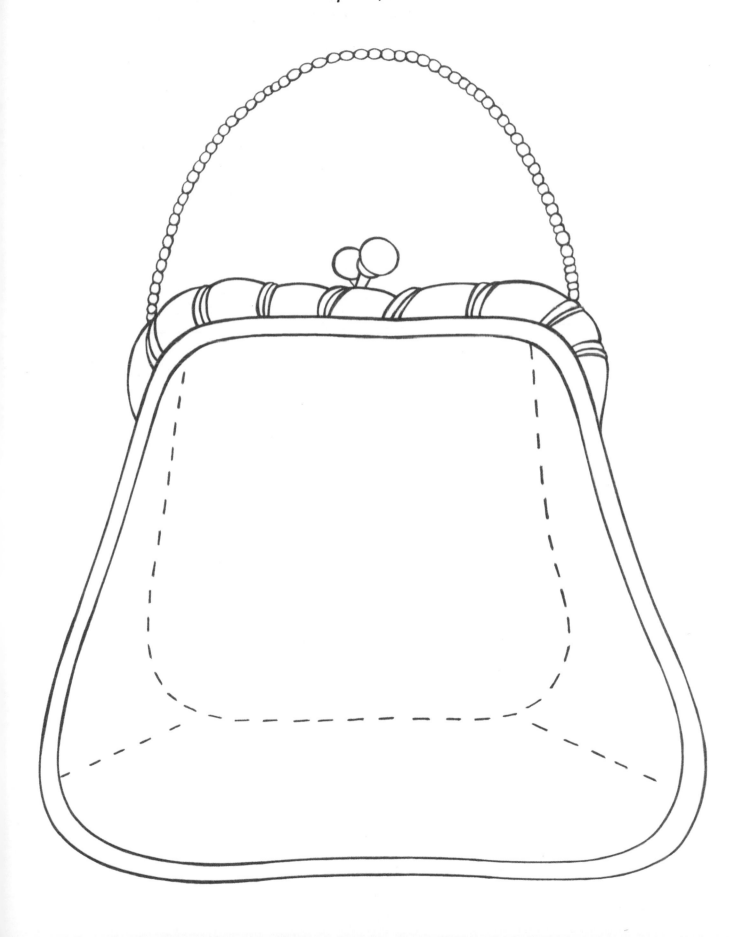

Pinkalicious Likes to Sing

Can you make up a song?
Write the words here.

Finish decorating the crowns
and circle the one you think
Pinkalicious should wear.

What Rhymes with Pink?

Write the words below.

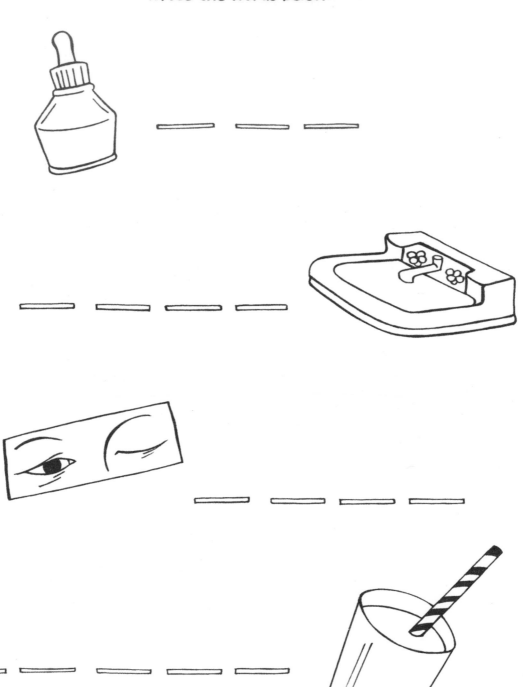

_ _ _ _

_ _ _ _

_ _ _ _

_ _ _ _ _

Draw your own magic wand,
and don't forget the ribbons!

If there were a Pinkadoodle breed of dog,
what would it look like?

Pink, Pink, Pink

Pinkerrific
Pinkatastic
Pinkerella
Pinkerbelle

Can you make up some other pink words?

Pink_____

Pink_____

Pink_____

Pink_____

Pink_____

Pink_____

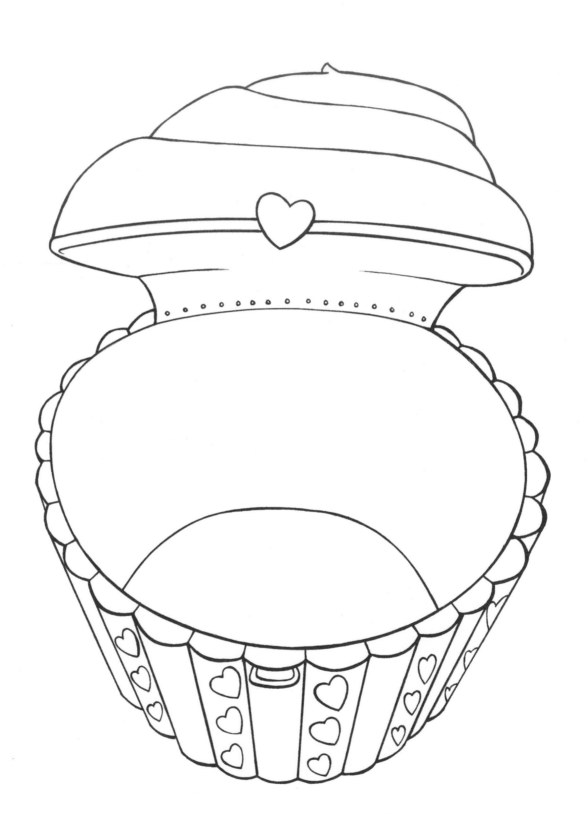

Add some jewelry!

Pinkadoodle!

What can you make out of these doodles?

Write a poem
about the color PINK!

Bubblicious!

Time for a bubble bath!
What is missing?
Finish the drawing.

When you take a bath,
what helps to get you clean?
Circle what you use.

Mommy is calling the pediatrician, Dr. Wink.
Can you connect the phone cord?

Finish decorating Dr. Wink's office.

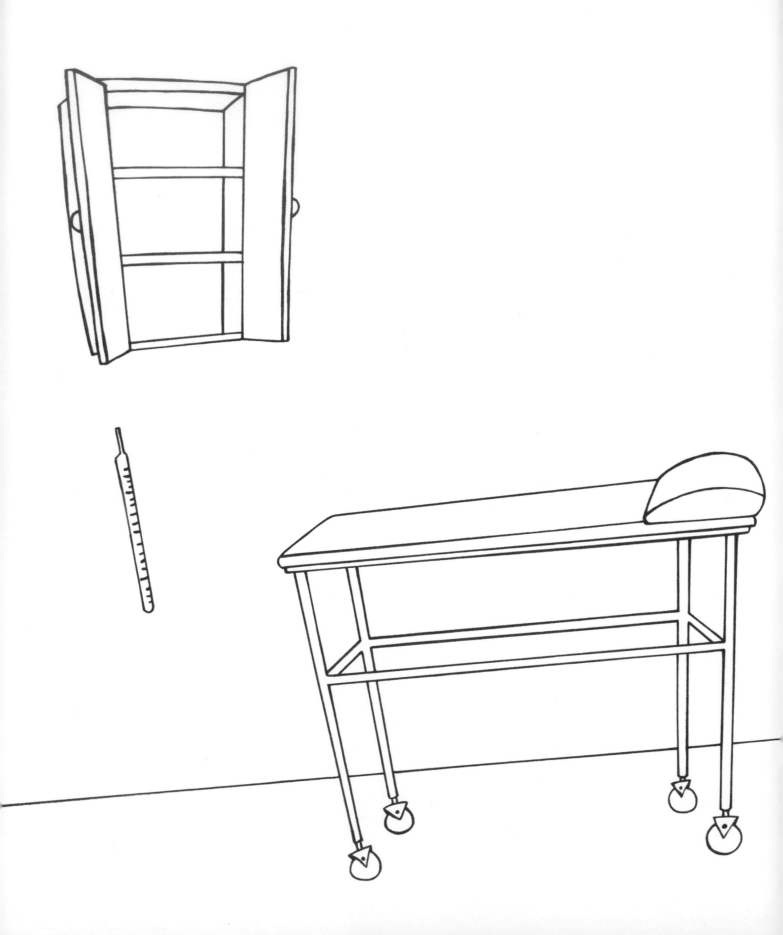

List three foods that you would NEVER eat.

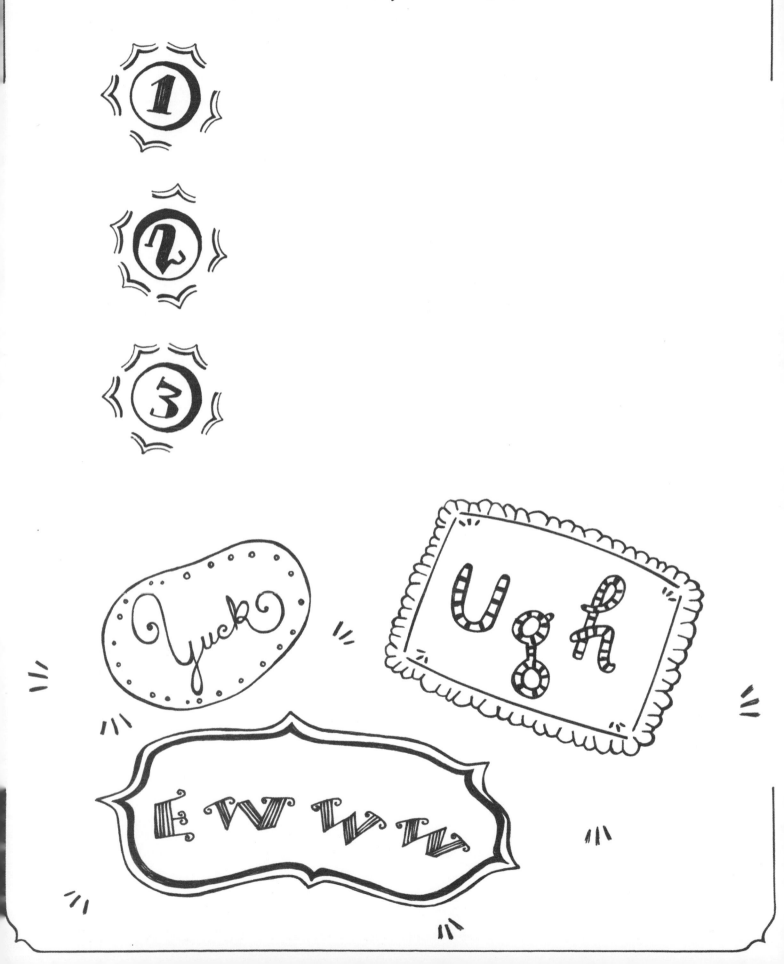

Color in the pink foods.
Now cross them out because Dr. Wink says,
"No more pink."

Mrs. Pinkerton needs a hat.
Draw five kinds of hats
and circle the one you like the most.

What would Mr. Pinkerton look like
if he had a mustache and beard?

Picnic Time

Finish this drawing.

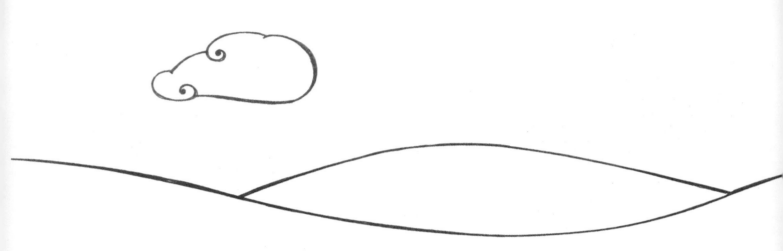

Draw the flowers in the park.

Which flower is different?

Draw your friends playing on the playground.

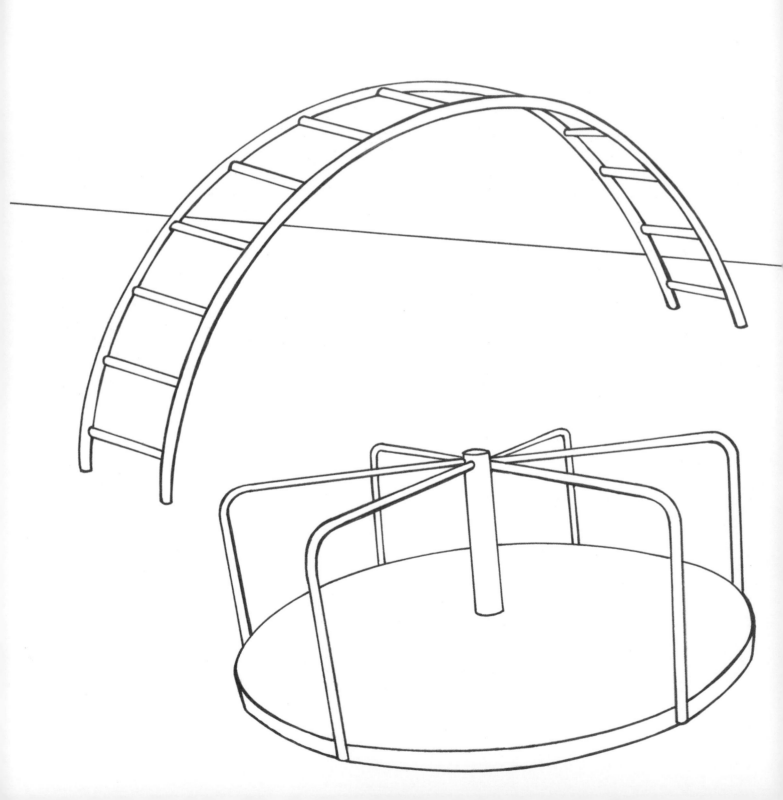

Draw a picture of yourself on the slide.

Peter likes the monkey bars!
Finish drawing in the bars so Peter can make it to the end.

Alison is Pinkalicious's friend.
Decorate her dress!

Draw a picture of you and your best friend.

Pink Riddle: Pinkadupertasticpinkerrific! How do you spell it?

What a perfectly pinkatastic day for the park.
Add some more butterflies, bees, and birds!

Pinkadoodle!

What can you make out of these loop-the-loops?

Draw Pinkalicious surrounded by bees, butterflies, and birds.

Help Pinkalicious, Peter, and Mrs. Pinkerton get home.

Start

Finish

Fill the bakery window with pinkatastic treats.

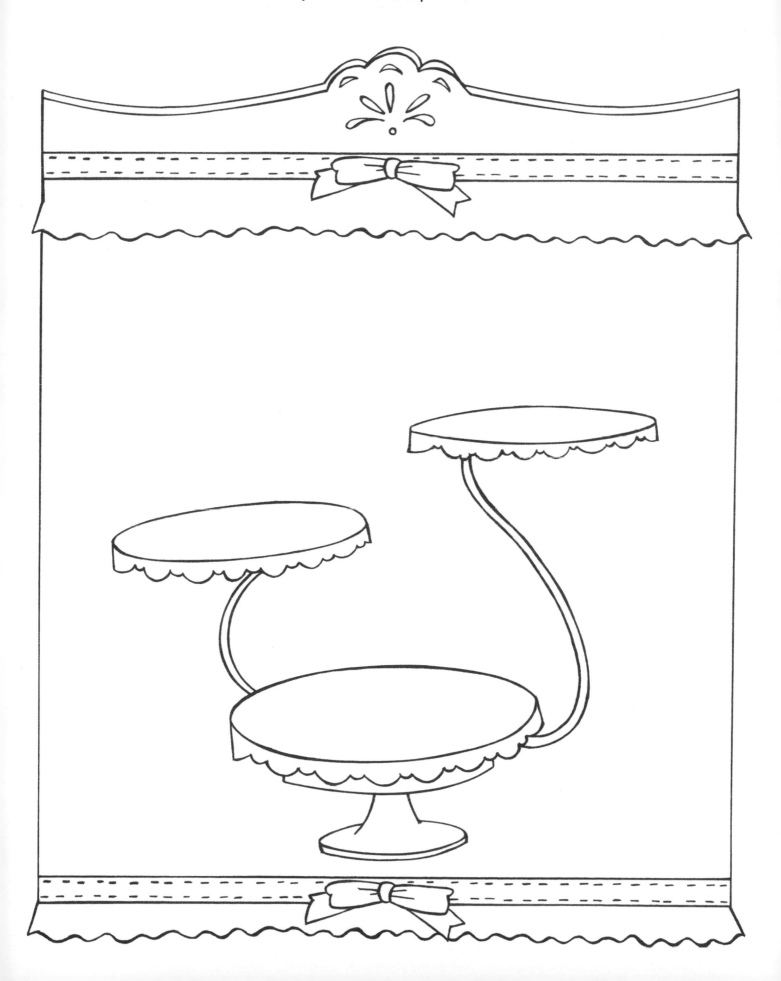

What is Peter daydreaming about?

Peter is green with envy.
He wishes that he were pink, too.
Finish the picture.

Pinkalicious has pinktails. Can you give her a new hairstyle?

Pinkadoodle!

What can you make out of these squiggles?

There are 12 hidden cupcakes in this room.
Can you find them?

Now that you have found the cupcakes, are you going to eat them?

Check the box with your answer.

☐ Yes, I will eat them all!

☐ I like to lick off all the frosting, but I don't eat the cake part. Does that count?

☐ I only eat the cake part.

☐ No, I won't eat them because I am a very good listener and I do only what my Mommy and Daddy ask me to do.

☐ No, I don't like cupcakes. I like ICE CREAM!

☐ Yes, I like EVERYTHING!

Pinkalicious has eaten so many cupcakes
she's turned from pink to red.
Finish the drawing and color it in.

Pinkatastic!

Draw what you would look like if you ate ALL the cupcakes!

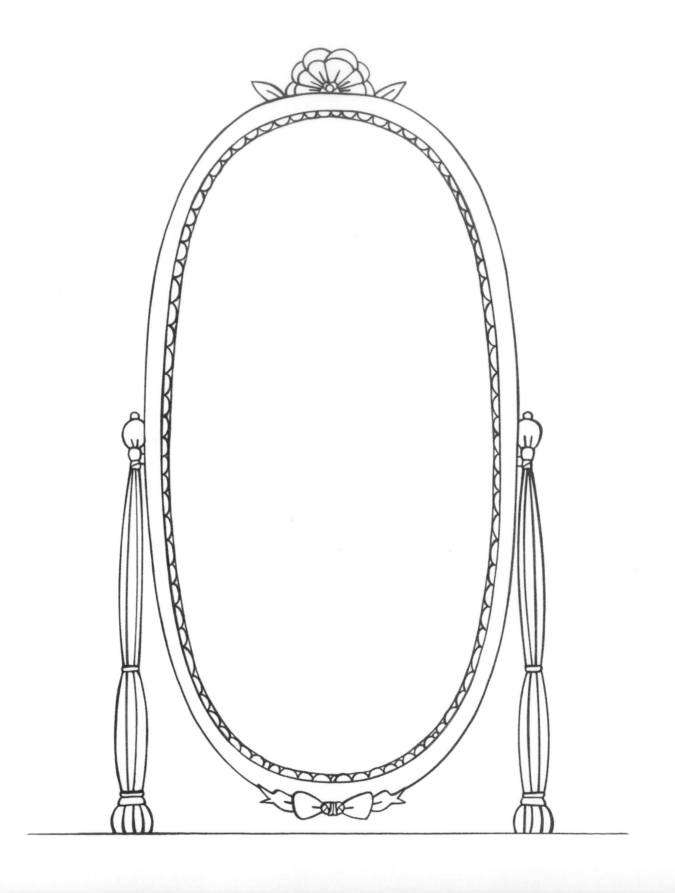

Pinkalicious has just remembered what Dr. Wink
told her about eating cupcakes. Do you remember, too?

Pinkalicious has to eat green foods to return to normal.
Can you help her?
Circle your favorite foods that are green.

Avocado

Green Pears

Cabbage

Napa Cabbage

Green Apple

Honeydew Melon

Asparagus

Kiwi

Green

Lime

Beans

Broccoli

Artichoke

Cucumber

Green

Grapes

Today's Menu

Appetizers

Salad

Entrée ♥

♥ Dessert

Peter and Pinkalicious are having a food fight.
Add more food.
What a mess!

Draw a dinner
made of green food.

Draw a picture of yourself doing an "I love green food" dance.

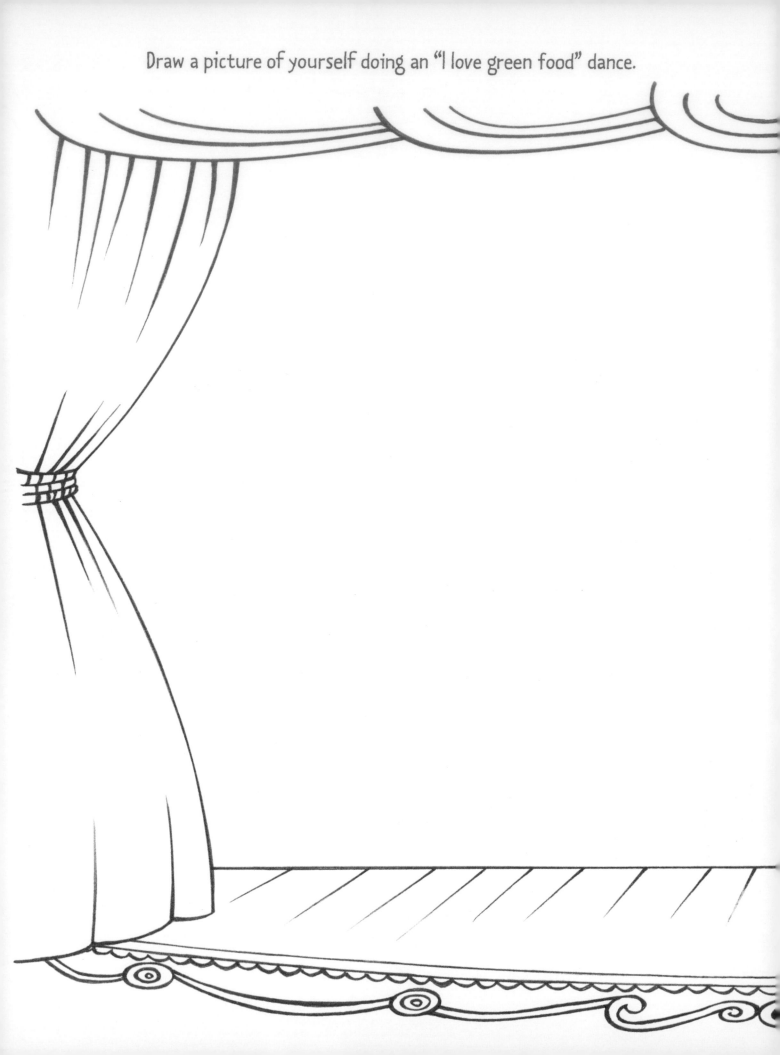

Complete this message
by connecting all the dashes.

I am me and
I am
beautiful

What does Pinkalicious see in the mirror?

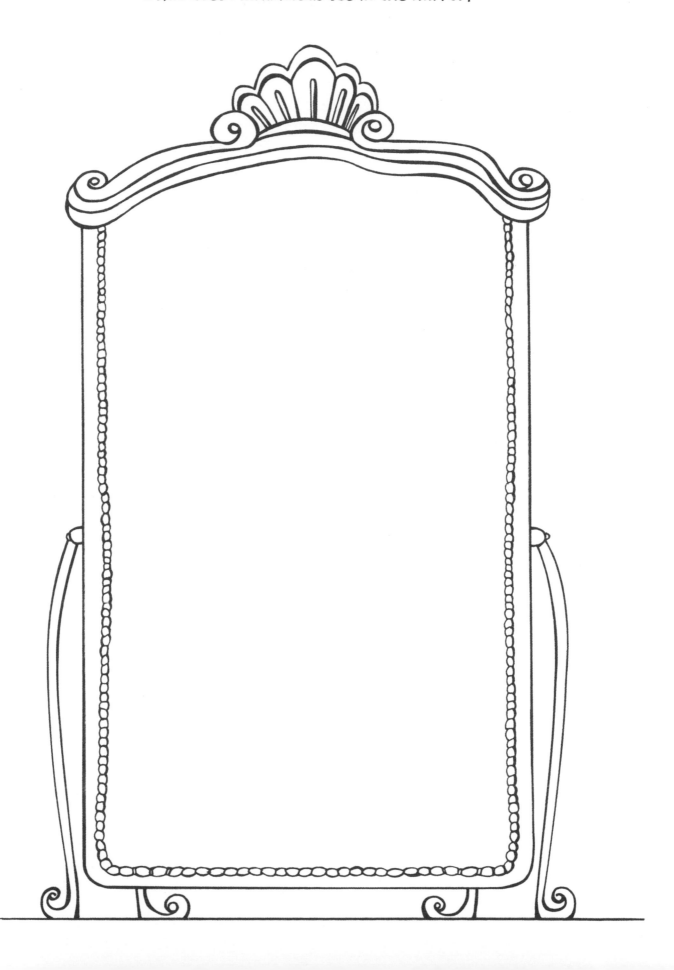

How does Pinkalicious feel?
Is she joyful?
Sad? Confused? Surprised?

Color in the drawing of Pinkalicious
when she returns to her normal color.

Look at all these cupcake wrappers!
Draw the person who ate all the cupcakes!
Was it you?

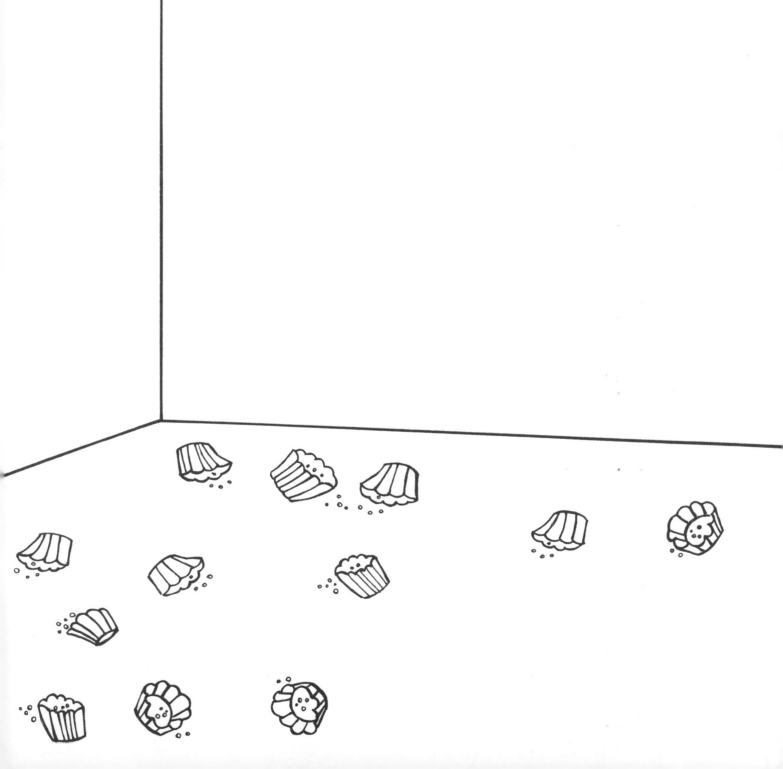

Pink-a-boo !

Peter ate too many cupcakes and now he is pink!
Color him in!

Connect the dots!

Six of My Favorite Things:

1. one ....

2. two ....

3. three ....

4. four ....

5. five ....

6. ....

I love this most in the world!

Use these pages for oodles of pinkadoodles.
Think pink!